I AM DARN TOUGH

Story by Licia Morelli

Illustrated by Maine Diaz

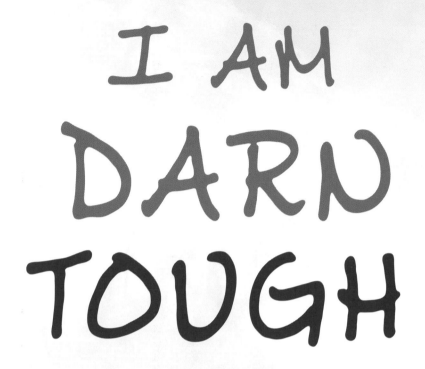

TILBURY HOUSE PUBLISHERS
THOMASTON, MAINE

I remember tying my shoes.

Sun on my skin.

Wind on my face.

I remember the crunch of the dirt beneath my sneakers.

My legs kicking up behind me.

Rocks. Roots.

I remember running through mud.
Puddles mirroring the trees around me.

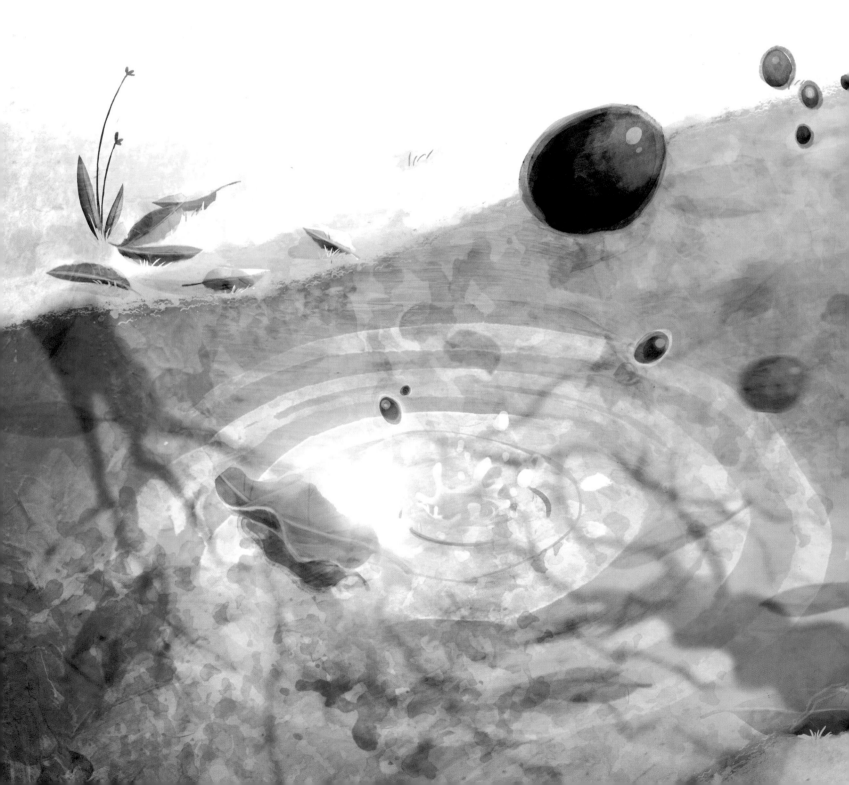

The babble of a stream.
Wind in the leaves above me.

I remember tripping and falling.

My knee bleeding.

Then slowly getting up.

Putting one foot in front of the other.

I remember that first big hill.
The climb up, up, up.

I remember a cramp in my side.

Being so tired. Muscles aching. The sun, so hot.

I remember crying, feeling defeated.

My heart hurting, stomach in knots.

I remember stopping.

Taking a deep breath in and out.

Telling myself that I've done this before,

and I can do it again.

My heart is big.

I am brave.

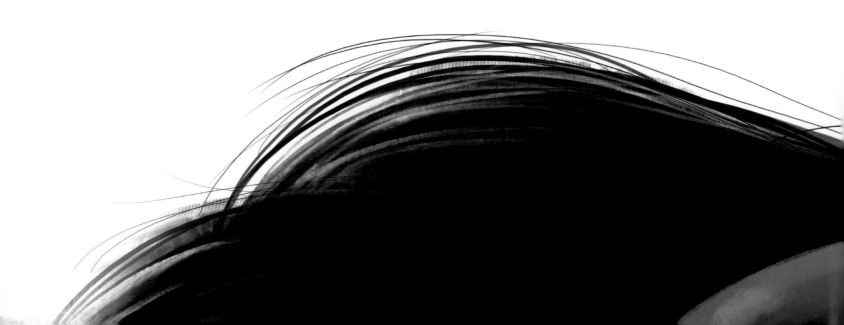

I remember the breeze at my back.

My feet bouncing on the trail.

The cramp going away.

I remember catching up to my friends.

Smiling. Laughing.

Cheering each other on.

I remember seeing the finish line.

Running through the tape, arms up!

Smiling so big—I did it! We did it!

I know now that I'm strong on the inside.

I'm strong on the outside.

I am darn tough.

Text © 2020 by Licia Morelli
Illustrations © 2020 by Maine Diaz

Hardcover ISBN 978-0-88448-780-7

Tilbury House Publishers
www.tilburyhouse.com

Library of Congress Control Number: 2020939610

Designed by Frame25 Productions
Printed in Korea

15 16 17 18 19 20 XXX 10 9 8 7 6 5 4 3 2 1

To Jed, Hollis, and Elsa, and
your big, tender hearts.
—L.M.

Licia Morelli is a writer whose essays and poetry have been featured in *Vanity Fair, The Rumpus, Johns Hopkins Press, Maine Media Workshops + College, ARTS Magazine*, and other publications. She believes that more people should trust their intuition and eat chocolate chip cookies, both of which inspire good writing. Licia is a mother of two children and the Maine Literary Award – winning author of *The Lemonade Hurricane* (Tilbury House, 2015).

Maine Diaz is a film animator and illustrator whose children's books have been published worldwide. She lives in Argentina.